EX LIBRIS
Velma Lucille
Gooch 1983

THE SHUNNING

Patrick Friesen

WINNIPEG: TURNSTONE PRESS, 1980

Canadian Cataloguing in Publication Data

Friesen, Patrick, 1946-
The shunning

Poems.
ISBN 0-88801-038-9

I. Title.
PS8561.R54S5 C811'.54 C80-091052-4
PR9199.3.F75S5

ISBN 0-88801-038-9

Cover design by Michael Olito

in memory of my grandfathers
Klaas Friesen 1881-1961
Jacob Sawatzky 1903-1979
my father
Franz Friesen 1916-1971
but also for my son Niko

This story concerns two brothers, Peter and Johannes Neufeld, and their families; Peter's wife Helena, Johann's wives Carolina and Ruth, and Johann's daughter Anna.

All diary entries are either those of Mrs. Hiebert, midwife, or of Dr. Blanchard, recently arrived from Orange County, Ontario.

There are numerous other characters, grandfathers and deacons and such, who do not say a word to us. An historian, who keeps time, has a thing or two to say.

All characters in this book are surely fictional.

some praise God
some cry uncle

I

his shunning

And they shall drive thee from men, and thy dwelling shall be with the beasts of the field. . .

August 12

A hundred and one things to do, but anyways Tina is getting a little better. Her fever is almost gone and she can swallow already.

Started canning today. Finished 12 quarts of yellow beans. The two oldest girls picked a lot of raspberries for preserves and jam. Maybe I can do all the beans tomorrow.

Old Mrs. Friesen, my aunt Katie, died yesterday. The Lord giveth and the Lord taketh away.

August 13

Abe Neufeld came with his buggy in the night. The boy was born around 6 in the morning. Their first boy. It was a very easy birth. The boy was skinny, though, and will be sickly. He has a big nose like his father. So far this year I have brought 5 children into this world. All were healthy.

I did the last of the beans today. Altogether there are 20 quarts. I finished the raspberry preserves too. There weren't many this year.

Tina eating again today.

he had disobeyed. had waded barefoot in the creek before the weather was warm enough. you could easy have got a cold she said. she brought out a spool of #10 thread and tied his ankle to a tree with a 5 foot length.

break that and you get strapping.

mother hoeing

her red arms
her eight-month belly
her hair tied into a knot

then the bright hoe raised high
slashing down like a sun
again   again
and mother stoops to pick up the mangled snake
slings it over the fence   a yellow rope

she wipes her hands on her apron
nostrils wrinkling she turns to me   smell this
I inhale the musk and grease of her hands

his mother thought it was the second coming   one taken   one left. her eye has wandered for a moment. when she turned back she alone stood in mid-garden   hoe in hand.

for that instant she stood bewildered. christ had returned and left her behind. that was not her horror   the taken son was. to lose her only child   the flesh she loved more than herself   the flesh that would be made word.

her eyes looked for directions in the garden   in the sky. there were no flames or winds. everything was still   as before   yet all lost in a moment.

then she saw corn stalks wave at garden's end. she ran to hug the boy with corn silk for his beard. a prodigal son   a kind of ghost   baffled by her love.

I asked father why the garden needed ploughing
and without thinking or raising his eyes
he said that for anything to grow the earth must be turned

somehow the unruly garden was always smooth and hard-packed
    by mid-summer
and somehow the carrots and potatoes always grew in rows

and sometimes I stopped playing
to watch father on his knees among the gladioli
only his hands moving   as if they were leaves the air breathed upon

long as I remember
someone listening at the door   or
crossing the yard beneath my window

mother peering between crib slats for my next breath
holding her breath for me as I dreamed

long as I remember   these people
open fields and the sun shaping a shadow of me
these people   staring
and merciless light

longing   as I remember
for night to blacken the sky

we climbed the hayloft
swallows skimmed out the door
we sat   feet hanging outside

father seeding a quarter-mile away

our creek shining in the sun
Peter said it was a silver S
a brand placed on earth by God

a hawk hanging high and black

swallows fluttered beneath eaves
their nests like pouches
Peter said they were purses holding gold coins
to pay the hawk as rent

red-winged blackbirds wagging on cattails
Peter said they were his favourite bird
they bleed but never die he said

and mother calling   as usual
to make sure we were all right

black horses
muzzles glittering with frost
chains like frozen chimes

black horses
dragging logs into the firelight
their shadows rear across trees

and I'm wide-eyed all night

voices shouting commands
echoing from farther forests
and no one in sight

and this is how I dream of emptiness

I latch the barn door
bend to pick up a pail of milk
then wobble through snowdrifts

a steel guitar cries from our house
I pause   the night below zero
and listen to Peter's nasal song

He lifted me up to a heavenly place

I look up   there
icy sheets of northern lights
planets reeling above the barn

only words sung   the guitar
encounter this star-marred night
and utter folly

Uncle Peter had the farm beside ours. I remember him as a quiet, serious man. He seemed never to be happy. I know I always admired Aunt Helen for being so patient with him, for taking him through the bad times. I was young then and I remember him from the time when he was having trouble with the church. So I guess there was a good reason for him being unhappy. That was a bad time. For us too. Mother and father were not supposed to visit Peter. I remember some men from church talking to father once for a long time.

People said Uncle Peter had too much pride. That's all I ever heard, and father wouldn't talk about it. Peter sure was his own man. That I know. You should have seen him walking behind his horses. Just the way he walked, ploughing or seeding, was kind of proud. You never saw him stooped, even when he carried heavy feed bags.

And you know, he was not a big man, quite thin even. He had kind of a hooked nose, I would say, and blue eyes, like the sky in summer, or sometimes greyish, also like the sky. Father, I remember, sometimes called him *der blaue Engel*. I always thought it was because of those eyes. It seemed a funny thing to call a man.

I remember now too that Uncle Peter had asthma. Especially in the winter, or on cold evenings in the fall, his breathing would get heavy and his voice scratchy. After an attack once he told me I didn't know how lucky I was to be able to breathe easily. Then, after he got his breath back, he sort of laughed and asked what I thought would happen to a fish that couldn't live in water.

Uncle Peter left people alone and he wanted to be left alone. He would go into the bush when he felt too strong about one thing or another. Like when he was angry. And you never saw a temper like his. I know about his temper because I sometimes sneaked up on him near Buffalo Field. You know when you're young with nothing to do and you roam around, finding out things? Well, I did that too, and I found the spot where Uncle Peter would walk back and forth when he was upset. Right on the edge of Buffalo Field.

Anyways, usually he was quiet. One time, though, he was swearing and punching a poplar tree with his fist. When I went to look at the tree after he had gone, there was blood smeared on the bark. I wouldn't have wanted to see his knuckles.

I guess mainly he just wanted grownups to leave him alone because he would let me help with his work. He would teach me to do things right. He did his work just right always and so quickly.

sometimes the sun glowers
burns me black into soil
so that I am Adam again   before sin
before creation's frenzy

Lord Jesus Christ breathe into me
make me man   make me flesh again
as God the Father did in the beginning
and take away all sin and shame

✓

a cry

of some animal caught

no (my son   stung
I spit on my fingers
salve the reddening bump
and he asking   will I die?

I'm thinking we all die

but he runs before I answer
no   he will not die yet
he is not a stranger to this earth)

woman   what does she want?
she knows the work I do   long hours
look at these hands
and the lines the sun has made at the corners of my eyes

what does she think the horses would do
if I didn't prop up the fence where it sags?
and the chickens   can they live on stones?
when do I find time for the garden?
as if I don't see enough of the sun
and when do I have a minute for my sweat to dry?

one day I'll give her an earful   straighten things out
what does she think a man can do in one day?
how many hours are there? am I not to sleep?

even these poplars know it's not easy
before she knows it I'll be bones too   like Queenie here
I may as well lie down right now
she can visit   lay flowers on me
let's see where the farm goes without me

at night she says she wants me for herself
one of these days she'll see how much of me is left

rivers

a woman sags in ropes
her hair seaweed

where horses ford
bridle and sword glinting

the river grandfather swims
naked in his slim strength

where mosquitoes cloud a paddlewheeler

these rivers flowing me back
and   as in a dream   I cross and cross

I kiss His hands His feet
and though my lips redden
I cannot taste His blood

to find love

to find love
I sit on the stone between tomb
and Christ risen   pale with hunger

to find Jesus   alone   in the garden
before the serpent crawls through the fence

child

his fine legs   bent at the knee
squeeze the horse
he hardly occupies the saddle
grasping pommel and mane
his hair like honey in the sun
brown eyes take everything in

the horse a white sculpture

father   his eyes slit by light
stands beside horse and child
one hand clutches a lead rope
the other circles the neck
as if ready to wrestle the horse down

I lean in the doorway. Loewen with Penner and Funk behind and below him stands on the top step of the porch. His clean white shirt is buttoned to the throat but one shoelace is undone dangles off the step.

Loewen holds a black Bible before him and though he knows the verse by memory he reads with his finger.

> *And I will give unto thee the keys of the kingdom of heaven: and whatsoever thou shalt bind on earth shall be bound in heaven: and whatsoever thou shalt loose on earth shall be loosed in heaven.*

I step out and close the door so mosquitoes won't get in. There is very little room so Loewen backs down right on Funk's foot moves up again until both Funk and Penner are on the bottom step. When he is settled on the second step he wets a finger and pages further into his Bible.

> *Know ye not that a little leaven leaveneth the whole lump? Purge out therefore the old leaven, that ye may be a new lump, as ye are unleavened.*

Penner slaps the back of one hand with the other. A tiny scarlet splash there and a wreckage of black legs and wings. Funk waves his hat back and forth in front of his face. There are mosquitoes on Loewen's hands one on his cheek but he pages on and reads.

> *It is a fearful thing to fall into the hands of the living God.*

Bible closes. They bow their heads and Loewen prays for my salvation and that they will do the right thing. I move toward Loewen as he prays. He backs down. Funk and Penner stumble off the porch. Loewen shuffles aside as I go down and walk to the barn.

it was july   and the sun
there was a *tsocka boum* and a rope swing
Peter sat upright   motionless
all afternoon he gazed unseeing across his land
everyone else was inside   Helena   the children

only

two horses   muzzle to muzzle
stand against the fence   tails flicking flies

Brummer   hot on the trail   yelping in the trees

and Peter on the swing

that sunday was the first day of his shunning

It was never easy to know Peter. I never had cause to doubt his love for me, but I didn't understand some of his ideas. He said more than once that there couldn't be such a place as hell, not with a loving God. That's what started all the trouble with the church. Peter must have mentioned this to someone and the pastor got to hear about it I guess.

The first time Reverend Loewen came over alone to talk with Peter. They didn't want me to listen, but I knew my Peter. He didn't change his mind, and I think that's where the talk of pride started. Things just got worse and worse. The more Loewen talked to Peter, the more stubborn he got.

He was banned. It was July. A very hot July and lots of mosquitoes. Loewen and two deacons talked to Peter at the front door. I remember Peter would not invite them in. He stood in the open door, letting in mosquitoes like crazy. Then Peter must have gone to the barn, and the three men asked if they could come in and talk to me.

I must not share our bed with Peter, they said. I would surely be damned if I did. Such matters were, of course, right only between husband and wife and only if they shared the true faith and were submissive to the church. Christ's bride.

This was very hard for me, to stay away from Peter. I loved him. I remembered our wedding, how I had vowed to submit myself to him. But he never pushed for it. He must have known what they told me, and he was so proud. He never asked to enter my bed.

We talked it over, and I was scared by what he had to say about the church. I told him that if he wasn't right with them something must be wrong. I said we should try it the way they said. For a while. And maybe he would find his way to a firm faith again. Maybe it would help him settle his doubts. Peter said nothing.

Of course he got worse when people stopped coming to get eggs. The eggs we couldn't use Peter threw on a pile beside the hen house. One morning he slaughtered all the hens. I don't want to say how he did it. I never knew people could do things like that. He hardly ever spoke to me anymore. We got farther apart. I wanted him, but I thought he was wrong. I thought he was wrong. And I did not want to lose my faith. My Christ.

the boys beg to help father pitch hay
peter hands them a hayfork
and stands aside   leaning on the fence
a bridle   a garter snake slung over the top rail

he pulls a red handkerchief from his back pocket
wipes his brow   blows his nose
boys   he laughs   that way it'll be christmas before you finish
all in one motion   using legs as well as arms
see   and he skims a forkful of hay from wagon to hayrick
not bending his back but turning at hip's fulcrum

helen calls her men for supper
peter unties a boot and shakes out chaff
he points at the darkening horizon
boys   see that   tomorrow it gives rain

Of course, father and Uncle Peter didn't once mention the shunning. How people no longer came to buy eggs or chickens. How, when Peter went to town to buy goods, the only people who would talk to him were Frenchmen he knew from La Broquerie. How even grandmother and grandfather had almost nothing to do with Peter. And how Helen was getting thinner and crowsfeet grew around her eyes. Instead they talked about last year's yield, this year's weather.

Even though they were pretty sure no one would be dropping in, I was told to watch at the front window.

Uncle Peter sort of half-lay in an overstuffed chair with one leg draped over the arm. This was not like Peter. But it was good to see him like that. Sitting there in one corner, not saying that much, but his eyes smiling. He looked the way I thought everyone should look on the day of rest.

Mother and Aunt Helen were in the kitchen making *vaspa.* Father talked and talked like he had saved up words for weeks. He talked about the stoneboat he had built, about the nuisance swallows were around the barn, about how he found the Heinrich Wiens boy killing crows with a slingshot then cutting off their legs for bounty.

I went for the kitchen, I remember. Heard mother saying that a woman owed her husband at least a little love even if she didn't feel like it. And Aunt Helen, nearly crying, saying it was not what she wanted but what they wanted. When the two heard me, Helen wiped her eyes with her apron, and mother said I should tell the men that the food was ready. At least if their hands were clean, it was.

her mouth's hungering held back
as she kisses my cheek at the doorway
then she is gone

I kneel to ease my belly's pain
strike my head on the floor
remembering her bare arms around me
how I went lost there
helpless as a baby
and I woke   a man again

forever   her flesh
and now winter

and memories can kill

where she is now   the church
hitching post
worn steps
the hard benches
and Helen
her black kerchief   her white face

sits apart   on fire

the snare tightens with struggle

I lie in bed
swaddled in moonlight
and someplace out there
a rabbit scrambles
shrilling   almost human in the snow
in raw december   in this lost year of our Lord 1914

if I could live
find something from my people
something to hold

the days that have fallen
that were months and years
when men broke the land
when women gave earth their children
when there was childhood
before the stoneboat   before the calloused hand

something to hold
from all those days going back

if I could find a love
that grabs Loewen by his collar and shakes him
awake   look again   look
with eyes open   see me   hands touch at least
at last a love that sloughs the flesh
and we are reborn in Christ   loving man

if I could know each day of our 400 years
take them in hand   and say   this is what it is

simply   something
to hold   to live for
to bring the kingdom here

and we   not forsaken

rooster crows the sun
and I know what must be done
before it crows again

I dress quickly
walk out   boots in hand

running for the henhouse
I smell the heap of smashed eggs
grab the startled rooster and twist his neck
throw him on the stinking eggs

hens flutter as I flounder   reaching
tearing with my hands   my teeth
spitting blood and feathers
fat headless hens dancing on broken shells
the room all dust and feathers
and my voice shaking rafters
my words sailing through walls
no   I bellow   no   no

and then it is still   so still

sun slants in at the windows
on the spattered floor   on my untied boots

from Johann's farm a cock crows
the sun will not be denied

this man less than a man
stands these days in doorways
this man my man I
flinch at this distance I have run

where fields grow bones
and nothing breathes
a graveyard I have circled before
now stumble stand in the middle
turning squint at the apparent edge the trees

this distance will not be forgiven

I must come back
sit on benches
if I am to be loved again

but how do I come back?

reverend loewen said his mouth was open. peter's mouth hung open
and he stared toward the trees. he didn't seem to hear loewen's words.
then   loewen remembered   peter said that he was cold.

all this light   he said
all this cold cold light

You know I didn't let go of Peter through all the trouble. Not even when he went wild that time. I finally let go when he was standing in the backyard, facing Reverend Loewen telling Peter how he could make things right again, how he could return to the church, how he could be with me again. Peter said nothing. I was washing the supper dishes and Peter in the backyard saying nothing. Just looking over Loewen's head toward the bush. When he finally said something, I saw his lips move, but all I heard was something about light. All the light, too much light, or something like that. Then Peter turned slowly to the kitchen window. I don't think he could see me. I was too far back from the screen. And he went to the barn. I let go.

forgive them   he whispers
limp hair and sweating
forgive them   he says
then his eyes open   ask why

of the world
mother weeps for him

his brother shivers at noon

a choir of soldiers sings   shoulder to shoulder

he smells rope at his wrists
the approaching rain

raises his head in the dark
forgive   he says
at last
me

I didn't see Peter leave the barn, but that wasn't unusual. Whenever he wanted to be alone, when he didn't want to be seen, Peter would go in the barn at the front and out through a back door. Then it was only a few steps into scrub bush. That barn was almost like a tunnel from the yard into bush.

What he did in the scrub I'm not sure. I saw him there only once. I was walking back from visiting my sister-in-law, Carolina. When I got to the clearing, we called it Buffalo Field because there were a lot of skulls and bones there, I saw Peter walking back and forth on the other side. He walked along the edge of the field, sometimes out of sight in the trees, then walking in sun. He didn't see me. I watched for maybe twenty minutes, and Peter just went in and out of the trees, the sun.

I was pretty sure Peter was in the scrub. This time I was worried because I had felt myself let go of him. Without deciding to do it I had let go. As if I had said "okay, you often go your own way. Now you can go forever because that's what you want even though you keep saying you love me."

When dishes were finished, I sat on the top step. Our boys, Henry and Leonard, were playing with Brummer, Johann's dog. They were throwing a stick, and he was fetching. It was still warm though it had rained in the day. The clouds were already going, and the sky over the trees grew red. The boys were singing "red sky at night, sailor's delight." I laughed and said "you mean farmer's delight," but they said no. It was "sailor's delight." I thought that here we are in the middle of scrub and, except for the Atlantic when our fathers came over, we haven't seen the ocean for four hundred years. Yet the boys are singing about "sailor's delight."

Then I remembered that father had once said that some of our people had been whalers back in the Lowlands. I couldn't believe it. These people crushing grain between thumb and forefinger for ripeness, pulling at a cow's teats, or picking chokecherries from stepladders, who could imagine them bending as the ship bucked, harpoon in hand, and Leviathan ahead spewing and snorting through wind and waves. Oh how I wished then for a sailor to come calling, to taste the salt on his lips. How I wanted to sail away with my sailor to warm lands. I was pretty silly then. I must have been about ten.

Now I was over thirty, and the red sky became night. I called the boys and put them to bed. I wondered where Peter was. I fell asleep on the couch waiting for him. I remember that I dreamed of sailing in an old ship. Someplace where gulls floated, rising and falling with the waves. When they tried to fly, they couldn't. The water held them. I felt so tired, trying to fly with them. I woke.

Peter was still not in the house so I lit a lantern and walked to the barn. No one there. I went to the henhouse. Empty. Just dark splotches, and feathers stuck to the floor.

Then I hurried back to the barn and went straight to the nails where Peter's .22 hung. But it wasn't there. I was not surprised. It was dark, and I knew I wouldn't find him. I went inside and sat up the rest of the night, my mind empty of anything.

I heard the rooster first. Then I heard Henry talking in his sleep. I woke him and asked if he was dreaming. I sent him for Johann.

I told Johann about Loewen being there last night and Peter not coming in for night. I said "find him, the rifle is gone, and he had nowhere to go."

a silver fall   water
fall arcing   aching
cock crow

singing the hollow

hallow
the hollow   singing

still
in that cold face
singing yes   yes   yes
singing   still
at cock crow
at caught cock crow
in the face of

no god
know

black wings flapping

in one appalling twitch
here beside this creek

blood spilling worthless
blood seeping in earth and heaven this night

where tomorrow

red sky

at morning
sailor's warning

the crouped child choking
and mother holding him over a steaming kettle

the child sprawled on gravel   licking his blood

the child   rolling his pantlegs to the knees
wading down twin creek   cattails bowing
this boy   his feet and calves mud-smeared
is man here   the caught corpse

one hand in water
one boot off   the other untied
his white foot nudging the rifle stock

his temple   a blue hole the bullet made

June 28

Blue jays woke me. A beautiful blue sky this morning.

While I was talking to Mrs. Dyck about her gall stones, my wife came in and whispered that someone had been shot. I rode out with Johann Neufeld. It was his brother who was dead. I asked how it had happened, and he said quietly that his brother shot himself.

He was lying in the bedroom. The cause of death was a gunshot wound to the right side of his head. We placed the body in the back of a wagon. The man's wife and young sons stood watching us. Neufeld brought the body into town. I filled out the papers in my office.

I'm puzzled by this suicide. I imagine it had something to do with his trouble with the church. Though what that trouble was I don't rightly understand. Strange people.

This evening I trimmed the lilac shrubs. Then I found this year's first ripe strawberries. Very tasty too. I had to go in because of the mosquitoes. They are awful this year.

Rereading Mill's *On Liberty*. Must reading for anyone claiming to be educated I would think.

living in another world
where mother lies stone cold
and father embraces us

living where the ghost is free

we were two boys
swaying in a *tsocka boum*

we chewed leaves and told the world's story
about the smell of rain   about blackbird's flying

two young men   courting women
you looking for someone to lose yourself in
I hunting for one that could make me shiver
and scent the rest of the world

but I almost forget   forgetting
that you were God's own
the kind of child that dies before he's grown

always out of breath

and I almost forget
you aiming a rifle at the sun
thinking you could bring night

we were two boys
like almost any others

Before Peter's death, in the months I slept alone, I was held in esteem. The leaders, like Loewen, praised me for my faith. In church I had the sympathy and respect of my brothers and sisters. I was being true to Christ. Some marvelled at my courage in living with a sinful man who had placed himself outside the church. They thought I feared and even despised Peter, but that I stayed in his house to give him a reason to come back to the Lord. I never feared him, though sometimes I feared for him. I loved him. They were right in thinking I was hoping to bring him back. But from where?

When he died something changed. They tried to comfort me by saying I had done what was best, that I had done the best I could for him. But very quickly they avoided me. Fewer and fewer women talked to me or, if they did, only in passing and about other things. They still said I had done God's will, but now I think they feared me. I felt sometimes like a witch.

And I lived in shame for many years. Maybe still. A shame that I had not behaved in a truly Christian way, in a human way, and that Peter had known and despaired for me. Johann called Peter *der blaue Engel*. Maybe we were two angels. I often thought Peter was not meant for this world. It could be that neither of us was. Though I am still here.

now his narrow home
a mound   a stone

wild rose bushes
barbed wire
and headstones on the other side

Franz Reimer
Katharina Plett
Bernhard Dyck

until the trumpet
until morning cracks open his grave
he lies apart
his face to the sun going down red

a part of them   Peter
who wanted so much what wasn't

if love could clothe his bones in flesh

II

time happens

For thou shalt be in league with the stones of the field: and the beasts of the field shall be at peace with thee.

Today. Everything just looks itself. No tricks. And the sounds   as if I tilted my head   banged it a few times with one hand   hopped on one leg and emptied my ear of water. I can hear again.

The horseshit   still steaming   even the horseshit smells sweet.

And those plums bending the branch   sweating juice where they split open. Their insides just busting to get out.

I tell you it's amazing. On these church steps   service over and sun bringing the afternoon. Hilderbrandt and Klassen comparing crops their wives deciding whose turn it is to visit. And Barkman over there   sitting on the rail   not talking at all. I think   if I know him at all   that he's remembering an afternoon like this   thirty years ago   when he could have tumbled a brown-eyed beauty   grey and lumpy now   five children   her husband's hands black from machines. Maybe he did. I've heard things.

But tell me something that tastes better than a strawberry. Something that makes your eyes squint and puckers your mouth. In July   when you're herding the cows home across Swallow Bridge and they turn off the dirt track to dip their muzzles in the creek   or like Peter used to say   when sun aims his bullets at us   is there anything you could want more than a handful of fat red strawberries?

Or this.

a woman walking home from church
her shawl loosens and slips to her shoulders
she pauses   removes combs and pins
lifts her face to the sky and shakes out her fiery hair

behind her the sun and golden withers
of a horse reaching for grass
beneath the bottom strand of barbed wire

a horse   the sun
and almost everyone shielding their eyes

on a sunday

thursday afternoon thunder
I come in from seeding
hoping to work other fields

and my Carolina's willing

I scrub at the basin
comb back my wet hair

cool air rustles at the window
we undress and stand
shivering   staring at flesh

the deep rift of her spine curving to buttocks
her fingers like feathers raising hairs on my arms
my flat stomach   her soft-bellied urge

Carolina takes my hand
and draws me beneath the quilt

I smell rain at the window

How she bunches freshly-cut gladioli in one quick hand and thrusts them into a pitcher. Her familiar fingers spreading the long stalks fluffing petals open.

How she walks   straight as a hollyhock   a milk-pail in each hand.

How she curves her head forward and to one side to watch the young one suck.

How like a girl she looks even though she is young.

rib-bones curving above grass
sun-painted skulls   like white wood
grained by wind and rain

these were cows and horses
carted here by Queenie or Bucky

chains around their hind legs
bloated bodies dragged into the weather

father's favorite   his first Prince
is bones here   his black hide his intestines
vanished like leaves   his stench lost in grass

my tongue tells names
and these bones speak their epitaph

a gopher rises
front legs at his chest
Brummer darts from my side
and suddenly nothing is there

November 21

The war is over in Europe but not here. Five of the patients I saw today have the flu. People are stunned by the ferocity of this epidemic. It is the invisible enemy.

It's been a long, wet fall. Today is cold, though, and an inch or more of snow has fallen.

November 22

Below zero today. The horses don't like this any better than I. They haven't grown a winter coat yet.

Since Mrs. Elizabeth Friesen and young Cornelius Siemens passed away on the 20th, there have been no new deaths. Henry Doerksen is over the worst. John Neufeld and his wife, however, are both seriously ill. Their daughter, Anna, and an aunt from Blumenort are taking care of the young children.

Tonight I read Carlyle. *Sartor Resartus. Doubt of any sort cannot be removed except by Action.*

November 23

The weather is clear and cold. I spread crumbs on the feeding stand for the sparrows. If I could be as hardy as they are.

November 24

Mrs. Neufeld passed away in the early morning. She was a young woman, only thirty-two, and left five young children. She had been asking for her children during the night. Apparently the youngest was at her breast and she stroking its hair. Her husband is unconscious. With their mother dead, the children need him now more than ever.

I read more Carlyle tonight.

Also repaired the door-jamb. Snow was drifting in.

My horses are worn out. J. Hiebert, my neighbour, offered the use of his team. I may have to take him up on that tomorrow.

to wake   finding november at the window
my wrist shrunk to bone
but to wake   again

earth   still fat with october
shivers beneath white wind

here   on this farm
between la broquerie and steinbach
now   in this hardening month   1918
they say she has gone
and though I hear myself say it isn't true
I know it is because the house is cold

I dream a blizzard

Barney and Prince flounder
snow whirling from treetops
spinning where wind twists one way then another
snow drifting to their chests
melting on muscle   forelegs driving
and wallow   and Barney strikes the rise where snow is thin
leans against a poplar   deadstill

I turn my eyes back to the hollow
snow rising like pillars as wind swoops
but there is no Prince
and when I look to the trees there is no Barney

snow fluttering against glass
and I'm wondering how hard the earth
shovels flashing at noon   iron strike iron
how they lowered her then
snow and dead leaves wheeling across her casket

I lie facedown on her side of the bed
the warmth   the musk of her
this I cannot bear

a mirror   face a stone behind glass
hanging there   almost silver   almost splintered
like a thin moon you can see through into dreams

eyes see themselves
everywhere they look

her hands grasp beneath armpits   wrinkling baby's skin
as she lifts the dripping child   (I remember

the towel   sea blue)   threads dangling
where it was torn from the larger cloth

she wipes her fingers on the apron

there is no getting away from the eyes
flat and cold
and the thin man   they show me
his mouth slack with staring
in his eyes are dreams to stun me

her legs open to land him
he flops at her breast   gaping
(I remember my dream of her
limbs flung   caught beneath a white sheet
I crawled in beside her   the fever of her flesh
vanished   only her cold skin against my lips

I remember our daughter crying in another room)

she straddles him on knees and palms
then lowers proudly to her elbows
he sucks at hungry nipples   (I remember
the child woke   I remember light from the other room
seeping in through a crack all around the door)

she stands sideways before the mirror
combing her hair with long fingers
half-sings   *mirror mirror on the wall*
then turns away laughing

at 2 a.m.
our daughter   suddenly awake
sways at the end of her bed
eyelids drooping   her eyes prowl the room
peering for the comfort of her mother's breast

her mouth remembers
and she listens for footsteps

I want to tell her about absence
how the mouth learns to crimp
I want to say that her mouth will know the world
and that sometimes she will hear silence

father will hold you   I say
and walk her past tears to sleep

Today one of the boys came running in calling "Mutti Mutti." He saw me at the stove stared for a moment. Sitting down he just looked at me a blue scarf around his forehead crossing his mouth and nose and wet where he breathed. Then he said "Papa come and see my snowman behind the house. It's finished." I put on my parka and went out to see. There it was three balls of snow one on top of the other branches for arms the eyes were coals. I said what a fine snowman but what are you going to call him? He thought then said "his name will be Johann yes if you give me one of your hats to put on his head he will be Johann."

When I was a young boy I once froze my feet. Father filled a tub with snow brought it in and began rubbing my feet with it. I remember how I cried. I said the snow hurt. Father said the snow made it hurt less. Nothing could take the pain away completely unless I wanted my feet to stay frozen. Then he said when the feet turned black they would have to be cut off with a crosscut saw.

january 21

neustadtgasse
narrow deserted
six men four in pairs two alone
sad men determined
too proud to crouch yet
walking cautiously in the shadows of houses
each man careful to walk in the tracks of the one who went before
and the tracks getting bigger their shapes vague

moonlight

(but I don't know this a dream
of facts or maybe a memory
I saw in my double tracks today
as I walked back from barn to house

remember?

yes the snow that's what
and the sound boots make in fresh snow)

snow squeaking
clouds of breath
a door opening light and the door closed
that's all

inside I don't remember a table? a candle?
or words muffled near the window?

it's dark
snow falls moonlight
filling my tracks between house and barn
this house alone
and me looking out

Loewen that same Loewen who spoke to Peter who spoke for the church with all the weight of the brotherhood behind him a brotherhood of brothers who would never condemn a man on their own who could almost all wash their hands and mourn Peter erring and falling Loewen died today beneath a load of logs. The logs were not yet properly fastened when the horses shied and broke the load. Maybe a bird near their feet they said or just something spooky in the air. And Loewen in red snow breathing his last a log across his chest. The men rolled one log off his legs but couldn't move the other before he sputtered blood and frozen air and died.

✓

to have you   to stem time
not when the camera blinked
and you bled in through its eye
but a moment before   you
standing among wild rose bushes
when you snatched a horsefly from the air
released it and turned into the photograph
squinting

curling at its edges
like paper   the yellowing moon
breaks when I touch it

like my red heart
like a leaf like dreams
the morning interrupts

I dream what was   apparently
a woman   almost thirty   hoeing weeds
a jar of water on a fencepost
her throat   as she drinks   a glass vase

and walking in a dream at noon   across the bridge
the white stroke of her arm
drops of water colliding silver with air
her hair dark and sleek   like an otter

eyes remember what was flesh
a dress brushing against russian thistles
shoes scuffing stones
a white finger bleeding from roses

I reach for the moon
to plant it like a seed
beside the porch   in the night
plant it and grow a sun
maybe   in the morning
a woman waking beside me

my wife lies quietly
so   just like we always did sleeping
yes   so beautiful   her shawl
roses on her black shawl
still   and still her violet eyes
and those worn hands   you wouldn't believe
how soft   soft   on my mouth
my eager mouth kissing   those fingers
those slender arms   those breasts

she moved with me   her hands on my hips
she twisted   we were so young   so
she twisted   spun on top of me   calling
Johann   Johann   she called me   she found me
yes   called in the night   through the whole world

we lay awake together
as winter tried to get in beneath the door
and that was long ago
we were young   even though
we were so young
things weren't always like that

black branches scrawled on air
a mumbling underfoot
and sun ringing in my ears

snow looks for a hole to crawl into
stalks bleed   bark swells and bursts
blasting winter to kingdom come

a time for thawing   that's for sure
a time to seed

easter's thorns
daffodils
hollyhocks leaning away from the house

I clear my throat
and begin to sing
softly   *amazing grace. . .*

how sweet the sound . . . brightshining
as the sun

I wasn't thinking of the child
swimming in the stone shell of her belly

I remembered cattle
how they lowed uneasily in labor
how scrawny legs stuck out like branches
how father tugged
as if he might tear the calf apart
how things were born   no matter what

no ceremony

only the animal butting into sight

I remembered smells
camphor or the slough
where the new one splashed   bawling like a calf

I remember the infant   her lank prince
animal or fish
wriggled at her breast
waiting pale-eyed for the waking kiss

I had been thinking of calling the child Franz. Carolina said why not call him Peter. But that's too much of a burden   to grow up with that name   to live with that story. At least that's what I said. I was thinking too that the name was unfinished   that somehow the name should be taken by someone and lived through until it was done. That name still had life in it.

It didn't seem fair though to ask this of a child. I kept my thoughts to myself. Carolina said that it would be an honour for the child after all Peter had been a good man who hadn't lived a false life only his own life. That made me think it over. Carolina was right Peter had lived his own life and maybe it was complete. Things couldn't have gone any differently. How could I say he was brave or not?

Well all the thinking and talking came to nothing. The child was a girl our Elizabeth. The full moon tonight makes me remember. I went outside after her birth. What seemed funny to me was that there were sundogs around the sun and Brummer was barking like crazy someplace in the fields.

Brummer howls me out of my dream. There is a sound like rain on the roof but light flickers at the window. Night begins to glow.

The boys are still asleep in the next room. I shake them awake and lower them from the window. Anna is already outside with the little one. Everyone is quiet. There is only the fire's crackle and Brummer howling.

Flames have hold of the summer kitchen and the porch where Brummer always sleeps. The boys are still half-asleep and try to crawl back through the window. I drop the pail I have just hauled from the well and run to pull them back. Anna stumbles across the ploughed field going for the neighbours.

Near the creek I cover the boys with horse blankets and tell them to sleep. And Brummer is quiet. I turn to the flames roaring like a wind fire stars floating on the night. Dog is dead I think I smell its burning flesh and my eyes all flames sparks shooting through my brain and Carolina dead just six months and shadows leaping against the barn. Voices somewhere. I break the kitchen window reaching in at the phone sill on fire the house buckling and me reaching to save the telephone. Flames at my arms my hair on fire I wrench the cord then I'm tumbling like a planet through heaven.

Father was rushing about. Getting the boys out of the way. He threw a few pails of water from the well onto the fire. He dragged the boys to the creek. He was shouting for Brummer to shut up. He was shouting "the dog can't get out, Brummer burns." I ran across the field with the youngest, my sister Elizabeth. I looked back over my shoulder and could see father's shadow running back and forth, and the flames rising higher, and the sky full of sparks. I left Elizabeth with Mrs. Plett and hurried back with Plett and two of his sons. Every part of the house was on fire now. At first I couldn't see father. Then I saw him standing at the edge of the fire, reaching through the kitchen window, and then falling in a fit. I got to him first, grabbed his ankles and pulled him to the middle of the yard. He was staring, his lips drawn back like a dog, and his legs trembling. In one hand that crazy man held our new telephone. We never figured out why he did that, and he never said.

After the fire? There's not much to say. When I fell it seemed that I fell through air. I never felt the ground.

I don't remember night after that. Only the morning ashes and beams leaning against each other. Anna sat beside me. The boys poked at the ruins with sticks and called Brummer. Maybe he's still alive they said.

I had no eyelashes. On my arms and head hair was melted into knots. Some hairs broke when I touched them. Anna said there had been fire on my head that she put out with her nightdress.

I felt there was something to say like after a dream and there's a story in your head you can't quite remember it but I hadn't dreamed and there was nothing to say.

Anna helped me to the creek. I knelt to wash my face stood up dripping brushed off ashes then saw for the first time I was naked. I laughed how I laughed. What a sight to have seen a wild man running around without clothes on fighting fire with a pail of water from the well.

Peter once told me that the stars were on fire. He knew a lot about stars about what shapes you could find at night. I don't know about stars burning they're still up there but that house is gone and the dog long buried.

the creek still flows every spring
though cattails have spread
and now as summer settles like dust
the water stands green and thick
slumbers through a memory of war

days flow too
and I wade downstream
ten years to the day
when I kneeled here
praying rushes to hold Peter
rock him tender until the sky opens

when I raised him pale as angels
and carried him home

here the spirit left flesh behind and ascended

here there is no forgetting
before he became broken man
the boy with yellow hair clothed in seasons

and here the blackbird
rising from a cattail
still bleeds

each spring I seed
and each summer the farm grows stones

if it doesn't make you cry   it makes you laugh

a cairn for each acre
or   from a distance   tombstones
nothing alive here but the horses
and me sweating for dirt   talking to myself

unload the stoneboat
make a living with what you have

One of my boys in the poplar tree at the end of the section. He thinks I can't see him. He's been there for an hour at least. I'll have to think of something for him to do. No   just pretend I don't see him. Next load   when I pass the tree   take out the axe like I'm going to chop the tree down. Let's see how long he keeps quiet that little snake in the grass.

hangs there like a cross   stiff-winged
between earth and sun
I bend to the stoneboat and forget
until his sudden shadow slides across the horses

I look up
he slants   braking descent with hard wings
his talons reaching   the animal twisting
and wings fanning dust
then he rises with the kill dangling broken-backed
an arch in the sky

Yellow storm all day   straw billowing like clouds. You had to stop sometimes and blow the dust from your nose. Wheels spinning   the belt turning round and round   shining black at midday. Your ears roaring   you could still hear it at night though the tractor was shut down   and I was feeding the machine   stooping and rising between the bandcutters' knives and the hungry machine.

And Ruth calling us to dinner. Ruth   an old maid with working hands. Ruth   who I'd known for years   who never married   and now Ruth standing at the pump asking if I would like to duck my head into the spouting water. I thought then she would be my wife   would share my life. Us growing old together.

Later she said to me that where I was   where my home was   her home would be.

So we married. And she was a good wife. We worked hard. She was a blessing to the children still at home. They had a mother. In the evenings we sat together. She would always be doing something with her hands   knitting maybe or mending. I guess I was remembering. And then   when I was remembering less   she gave me her gift. She gave me back feelings I thought I had buried. And she gave me a daughter. From our bed a daughter. It was a little while yet before we grew old together.

mother washing dishes
her head turned slightly
so she can hear what we're saying in the living room

father's birthday
and he's sitting in his proud chair
holding forth

and you know what that means

he and Henry Penner   stark naked
hanging onto their horses
swimming some russian river

that story

or Henry untying the neighbour's team
the neighbour being in the store
and father throwing stones
until the horses bolt
potatos flying from the wagon   scattering along the street

that story too

and the one about the Jew who borrowed a raincoat

but I know stories as well
though I don't have 75 years to remember from

The Jewish pedlar Feldman making his regular trip to New Bothwell carrying everything from thread to oilcloth and even tobacco for the Frenchmen. The sun is setting and Feldman begins packing up. Jake L. Barkman's boy Nick not even 20 years old sidles up to the Jew and says he has a confession to make.

Feldman looks up then goes back to packing. Maybe you want the priest from St. Pierre he says I don't take confessions though I can give you a good price on broadcloth for a suit. This flusters Barkman's boy and he says it isn't a joking matter. Feldman figures it must be something pretty serious then because most things you can laugh about.

Two years ago the boy says I stole a can of chewing tobacco from you. I have since made things right with the Lord. I am a different man now and want to ask your forgiveness. Who am I to forgive you asks Feldman you've made things right with God you say? Yah but I need your forgiveness as well. You're forgiven says the Jew. But that's not enough for Barkman's boy. He wants to pay for what he stole. How much do I owe he asks. Well sighs Feldman if you want to pay me a can of Red Man is worth 10¢ to me. 10¢? How about a nickel?

the house floating across fields
rain in sheets   clattering on windows
then shifting abruptly with the wind and the house still
black clouds roil   twist like fish
the bulk of whales sounding   rising
water sprays through the screen

I close the inside door   turn
to Ruth reaching a hand for me
smiling   she loosens a plait of hair with her free hand
I undo buttons slowly
her plump breasts   her breathing beneath the cloth

the dress falls to her waist
we nuzzle
my fingers trace her fleshy hips

we crawl under the old blanket

her toes wiggle   tickling my feet
our legs entwined like vines
her hair smelling of cloves

what else can one do but make warmth

rocking easily in the verandah
my eyes closed

the sun   flies buzzing
and the chair squeaking each time it rocks back

of a sudden my mouth wrinkles   my tongue squirms
as I bite and juice trickles

I open my eyes   light
and Ruth   her apron full of raspberries

old woman

I have known you always
even when you were someone else

the swirl of your dress
as you turn angrily from me
your eyes growing big and soft
when you make ready to cry

your body that seems too thick sometimes
and the hair too grey
so that I wonder how you looked when you were young

but youth lies in the grave

and I know   though you never say
that you don't like the stubble on my chin
I don't have all my teeth
my cheeks are hollow   and not all my hairs have stayed with me

yes   old woman   there is not much to choose between us
there are no others for you or me

I know

your calloused hands on the hoe
your arms around me

the grass grows too long around the house   let it
and if there is no time to paint the barn
well   that's one job less

When Aaron and I got married, there was a supper at my in-laws, the Reimers. Both our families were there.

My father-in-law, Klaas, now there was a rare man. He didn't know his real father, that I know. Much else, even his children didn't know. He would talk of his mother, her hard life, her family, but never of his father. You know, as well as I do, there are different kinds of fathers.

I heard awful stories, that when Klaas was a baby, just months old, his father held a shotgun to him. I guess he got talked out of it, or something. He ran away after that, the father did, and was never heard of again.

Klaas's mother, though, woke up one morning when she was in her fifties, and said that now her husband was dead. She had dreamed, saw her husband lying in a ditch beside a railroad track.

From such a start Klaas didn't grow the same as other boys. I've heard that most of the children could not play with him because he had no father. I guess, too, because his mother didn't seem too sorry. So are the sins of the fathers visited upon their sons.

Klaas was a dreamer, cut towns and animals out of paper. He didn't even play the usual games. Klaas told me of his only try at baseball. Someone gave him a mitt and stood him in the field among the gopher holes and cowpies. When the ball was hit his way, he said, all he could see was the sun. And that sun came down faster and faster, and Klaas forgot to lift his mitt. The ball struck him on the forehead. He said he dropped that mitt and walked home.

Anyways, I could keep telling stories. Klaas was a wise man, a quiet, dignified kind of man with white hair. Yet he liked to laugh and tell stories. I heard him tell my first boy about an Indian ghost that flew backwards. Don't ask me where he got such an idea or what it meant.

He was short, and I think that's why he tilted his head back a little, so he could look people in the eye. I remember, too, that he liked to come over on Monday mornings to eat chocolate cake left over from Sunday.

What I wanted to say was something else. Let's see. It was about our wedding supper. Oh yes. Klaas. How I always wanted to make a good impression on him. He had shelves full of books in both German and English, although lots of those were cowboy stories. But he spoke very clearly, very exactly. I was always careful in talking with him, to say things right. Although he only had grade eight, or something like that, he seemed quite educated.

My father, though, didn't care what impression he gave, as usual. I expected him to be himself. Laughing at the wrong times, and such a cackle like you can't imagine. Eating with his fingers because food tastes better with a little salt, or so he said. But what I didn't expect was for him to make a crude joke in front of everyone while we were eating.

Klaas was talking about the CNR and wondering why it didn't stop near father's farm. After all, he said, there was a sawmill in the area and a pretty big dairy farm. Father said that the train didn't stop exactly because of the dairy farm. He said there's too much cowshit, that's what he said, too much cowshit on the tracks and, when the train tries to stop, it just slides right by and doesn't stop till it gets to Giroux.

It was the most embarrassed I had ever been, and I quickly told father he shouldn't talk like that. Like what he asked. My face was beet-red. I looked at Klaas and saw that he really enjoyed what was going on. Not just the joke, but my embarrassment. Those two men got along just fine.

What do you want to know about Mennonites? What don't you know? Do you want to know about good people or not such good ones? Do you want to know about those that went to Africa or Asia to save the souls of heathens? Or do you want to hear about the quiet ones who live their faith so you never really notice until they're dead?

I can tell you about my daughter who was a nurse until she got married. She always lived for others. Even when she was a little girl she saved every cent she got her hands on. Not to buy something nice for herself but to send to missionaries. Always doing what she thought was best for others.

I can tell you also about the son that never learned anything from me especially about farming. Yet he has some kind of farm. His sons and his wife break their backs to keep the farm going. He drives to town every day for coffee. Sitting around with his cronies telling stories and jokes. I don't know what's in his head.

You know about some of our businessmen. The sharp ones who pay their workers dirt. Who live in their big houses and say God has blessed them. I always thought we were to share give our only coat to the man without one. We were to build a heavenly mansion not an earthly one. Yet I have heard one of these sharpies boast about how he gives work to the poor. That's sharing for him I guess. I sometimes wonder if these sharpies know where they would be without workers. You see how I don't understand things anymore.

ukraine
poland
netherlands
belgium
switzerland

from the shed blood of
Manz
Eberle
from Blaurock   his blue coat flapping at the knees
from lonely Denck   who believed that love would never hurt
from Pastor Philips
from Simons   running   hiding behind his priestly collar
from Grebel   on neustadtgasse

and we've come from rivers
rat
red
molotszhna   where father used to swim
rhine
limat   that swallowed a few of us

You can read about those things in books. I've read some but mostly what I know has been told to me or I have heard in sermons. Lots of countries and names. Sea of Galilee Palestine Beersheba Babylon Dead Sea Absalom Elijah Job. And don't forget it all comes down to Jesus. Not just for us. For the Frenchman too and the Englishman. For the Jew, God's chosen.

And do you understand we've come from memories?

simlins cowshit fires
horses wandering home through blizzards
Toews or Reimer frozen in the sleigh
grasshoppers in plagues
those born on oceans those buried there
steppes that father often talked of
with their yellow waves of wheat
the swamps of danzig where no armies could come
whaling ships yes whaling ships
and some of our people sailors
horse and foot blade flame and iron
those driven from home
and there being bears in the mountains
and soldiers in the countryside

do you understand?

those are my memories father's
his mother's maybe her mother father
their friends their neighbours

here in the brush by this creek where the limat flows
an overgrown orchard near poltava
or a wharf smelling of fish

do you understand this? where we came from?
it all adds up
figure it out for yourself

You say you've read about Simons. Now what do you know about him? Do you remember J.J. Fast? No of course not. You were only a boy when he died. But if you had known him you would know something about Simons. Fast was a blacksmith one of the last but he was just like Simons. That kind of man. Always serious. Even the few jokes he cracked weighed a ton. What mattered most to him more than his family I think was that the church should always be right that no one put himself above the church. And you never saw someone who could hide better. Behind the preacher. Behind the Bible. Behind God. Yes if you knew that man you knew something about Mennonites. Not everything mind you.

We had the telephone father saved when the house burned. But father would not get a car. Well, actually, he bought a Model A, but after trying it once, running through a flower garden, and finally stopping in the pig pen, boards all over and pigs squealing like crazy, he parked it and it didn't move again until years later when someone bought it as an antique.

He would not have a car. It's not that it was a sin. Father simply thought it was not the way for him to get from one place to another. He had his horses and that was good enough. Horses didn't make all that noise. Horses listened, and you could talk to them. You had to feed them, and they had a familiar smell.

Towards the end, when he wasn't strong anymore, we worried about him going to town with the wagon. He moved to town then. He was already not very well, and so he didn't last long.

MEDICAL RECORD

NAME John Neufeld

ADDRESS Sundown Lodge PH. NO. 29-1-2

RELIGION ~~German~~ Protestant RACE Canadian (German)

NEXT OF KIN Ruth Neufeld RELATIONSHIP Wife

ADDRESS Sundown Lodge

FAMILY PHYSICIAN

INFECTIOUS DISEASES None

ILLNESSES, ACCIDENTS, OPERATIONS Scars from burns (forearms); seizure disorder. Admitted under staff. Fatigue. Frequent shortness of breath. Indications of cyanosis, tachycardia, edema of the feet. Hb. 16 g%
W.B.C. 9 x 10^3 c. mm.
Urinalysis - normal. X-rays indicate pulmonary congestion and cardiac enlargement. EKG - L.V. enlargement
Medication - Digoxin 0.25 mg. daily, mersalyl 2 cc. i.m. daily -

A/

Anna brought me here. She and Aaron were visiting. They said I didn't look good. I told them they didn't need to tell me. I've known that since I was a boy when I first looked in a mirror. They said I couldn't take care of myself anymore. Anything might happen they said I might fall and break a leg and I wouldn't be found for days. Well maybe you should visit oftener I said but of course I was joking because they came often. Sometimes it seemed too often.

So it went. Then the next day a Monday and I was feeding the pigs slop there they were saying I could have a nice room in the old folks home. People would take care of me and I would be closer to Ruth. She was in the hospital because of her circulation. I think they were a bit embarrassed that their old father drove to town twice a week with wagon and horses to visit mother.

They were sure it was for my good. I would never stay at their place that would be too much of a burden besides Anna would always make sure I ate the right things so I packed one suitcase and went with them. They said they would pack everything else later. That's how fast it went. One minute feeding the pigs and the next in their '55 Chev looking back at that old grey barn leaning into the wind the tires bumping over the loose planks on Swallow Bridge.

It wasn't just a room. There were three little rooms. Ruth would soon be out of the hospital to live with me. But before she came Anna took me away again this time to the hospital. I guess I was a little weak. Anyway a doctor came to see me and said I should be in the hospital for a little while at least. The funny thing is that I had been in only one day when Ruth was sent to our new rooms. I never even saw her in the hospital.

Maybe I'll be better soon so I can live with Ruth in those rooms. Maybe I'll have to stay here. I don't know. One thing I know that farm is finished for me. Already it's sold pigs chickens horses and all. Some things they kept the children. A kerosene lamp some harnesses to hang on the basement wall and other junk.

I don't know how the world works anymore. How I got here so fast. And not even sick really. I wanted to fight them but that wouldn't do any good. They're younger probably know better than me what to do. Anyways that's the least I could do for them. Let them do what they think is best. I don't want to be on their conscience even if I don't understand what they're thinking.

Time happens. That's what. I wonder about Barney and Prince. No one uses horses for work anymore and that's all those two know. I wonder who bought them and for what. Anna says they're being looked after. About everything else well I don't think about it much anymore. The creek was pretty well dried up and the buildings falling so there's not much there. Just some things to remember. That's how it goes. You live a while and then time happens.

there's so much I could say about the old man his knobbly hands lying on the white sheet blue almost grey ridges of blood running across his hand's map his thin arms the pale blue top nurses tied in bows at his back his brown eyes you could see through if you weren't afraid.

he had nothing to say most of the time.

I rubbed his feet as if I could bring them warmth. I wanted to. he smiled looked through venetian blinds. the room was hot tight. near the window a water glass and the sun revealing his fingerprints.

what time he asked.

6:15.

I mean what year he said. then turned on his side still looking out the window.

tomorrow gives rain.

the ground he chose   to kneel
where he kneeled in mud
where he began to untie his boots
shivering   his hands shaking
and the sun settling in the grass

I know him   not well enough
I know his overalls were wet from knees to cuffs
his eyes were blue
I know he carried a poplar branch to goad the trigger

soft eyes   I think
soft eyes and blue as if the sky bled them

what he smelled at last
water rotting in the reeds
or air sweet with clover

what he saw at dusk
light walking away across fields
the hole a sky can be
what he saw   water rippling in a ring

brummer barking in the trees somewhere

the man johann
who fished here with a crooked nail he said
who splashed in this creek with his woman
when the sun was high and work could wait
johann who told how they ducked each other
how they swam underwater and exploded through the surface near
    drinking cows
the cattle lurching front legs in water
backing up the bank their large heads swaying

the flames he endured the iron in him

johann   I remember   leaning against a fence
his bony hands gesturing as he spoke

around us the wreckage of his farm
a rusting harrow   bone buildings careening
grass surging against the barn

johann remembered his brother
who tore the curtain and went blind
who taught johann fear   and not fear
that the child dies no matter what
and a man carries his funeral with him
you never know how many people you bury with a man
nor how many are born again

come   said johann   let's go back to the house
ruth bakes bread today
it's good when it's still warm and the butter melts

listen   he whispered

that rasping sound   that's a yellowhead
see it   over there   near the creek

and I saw
a blackbird with a sun for its head

O dass ich tausend Zungen hätte

der blaue Engel—German for "the blue angel."

tsocka boum—Low German name for maple tree. Literal translation—sugar tree.

vaspa—Low German word for the light, late-afternoon lunch, replacing supper on Sundays.

o dass ich tausend Zungen hätte—O that I had a thousand tongues—from a German hymn.

ACKNOWLEDGEMENTS

A brief extract from this book appeared in the *Mennonite Mirror.*

I am grateful to the Brock Street bunch, people like Ralph Friesen, Roy Vogt, Al Reimer, Ruth Vogt, Hannah Friesen, Jack Thiessen and the thin man;

Richard Hildebrandt in whose house most of this book was written;

Holly Richter and Alex Wilson who provided medical information;

Brenda Yakir for a story;

Robert Kroetsch for encouragement;

David Arnason and Robert Enright for editorial advice;

Webers, Brigitte and Werner, who gave me their fine house on Sturgeon Creek for a few weeks in 1978.

Special appreciation for the Manitoba Arts Council and their major grant which allowed me to write freely for the winter of 1978/79.

Front cover photo, and photos on pages 7 and 101, are from the Manitoba Provincial Archives. Back cover photo of Patrick Friesen by Allan Kroeker. Large back cover photo, and photos on pages 53 and 54, are from Patrick Friesen's collection.

Turnstone Press
The Shunning
by Patrick Friesen

Turnstone Press gratefully acknowledges the support of the Multiculturalism Program, Government of Canada, which has aided in the publication of this book.

Turnstone Press
St. John's College
University of Manitoba
Winnipeg, Manitoba
R3T 2M5

Books by Turnstone Press

In the Gutting Shed by W.D. Valgardson
Open Country by George Amabile
the lands I am by Patrick Friesen
Changehouse by Michael Tregebov
Seems Valuable by Ed Upward
Seed Catalogue by Robert Kroetsch
The Inside Animal by Arthur Adamson
Blowing Dust off the Lens by Jim Wallace
bluebottle by Patrick Friesen
Soviet Poems by Ralph Gustafson
Rehearsal for Dancers by Craig Powell
Mister Never by Miriam Waddington
The Cranberry Tree by Enid Delgatty Rutland
Rock Painter by R.E. Rashley
First Ghost to Canada by Kenneth McRobbie
No Longer Two People by Patrick Lane and Lorna Uher
The Earth Is One Body by David Waltner-Toews
The Man with the Styrofoam Head by Gregory Grace
When the Dogs Bark at Night by Valerie Reed
The Bridge, That Summer by A.E. Ammeter
This Body That I Live In by Anne Le Dressay
Mother's Gone Fishing by Norma Dillon
Almost a Ritual by Les Siemieniuk
Jimmy Bang Poems by Victor Enns
Across the White Lawn by Robert Foster
Shore Lines by Douglas Barbour
No Country for White Men by Gordon Turner
Interstices of Night by Terrence Heath
A Planet Mostly Sea by Tom Wayman
Scarecrow by Douglas Smith
Leaving by Dennis Cooley
The Light of Our Bones by Douglas Smith
Settlement Poems 1 by Kristjana Gunnars
I Want to Tell You Lies by John Lane
Marsh Burning by David Arnason